THE TALE OF TOM KITTEN™

Based on the original and authorized story
by Beatrix Potter
Ladybird Books in association with Frederick Warne

Once upon a time there were three little kittens, and their names were Mittens, Tom Kitten and Moppet. They often used to tumble about and play in the dust.

Ladybird books are widely available, but in case of
difficulty may be ordered by post or telephone from:

Ladybird Books – Cash Sales Department
Littlegate Road Paignton Devon TQ3 3BE
Telephone 0803 554761

A catalogue record for this book is available
from the British Library

Published by Ladybird Books Ltd Loughborough Leicestershire UK
Ladybird Books Inc Auburn Maine 04210 USA

One day, their mother – Mrs Tabitha
Twitchit – expected friends to tea, so
she fetched the kittens indoors, to
wash and dress them before the fine
company arrived.

First she scrubbed their faces. Then she brushed their fur. Then she combed their tails and whiskers. Tom was very naughty and he scratched.

Mrs Tabitha Twitchit dressed Moppet
and Mittens in clean pinafores and
tuckers.

Then she took all sorts of elegant uncomfortable clothes out of a chest of drawers in order to dress up her son Thomas.

Tom Kitten was very fat and he had
grown. Several buttons burst off his
jacket. His mother sewed them on
again.

When the three kittens were ready,
Mrs Tabitha Twitchit unwisely turned
them out into the garden to be out of
the way while she made hot buttered
toast.

"Now keep your frocks clean, children!" she called. "You must walk on your hind legs. Keep away from the dirty ash-pit. And from Sally Henny Penny, and from the pig-sty, and the Puddle-Ducks."

Moppet and Mittens walked down the garden path unsteadily. Presently they trod upon their pinafores and fell on their noses. When they stood up there were several green smears on their clothes!

"Let's climb up the rockery, and sit on the garden wall," said Moppet.

They turned their pinafores back to front and went up with a skip and a jump.

Moppet's white tucker fell down into the road.

Tom Kitten was quite unable to jump when walking on his hind legs in trousers. He came up the rockery by degrees, breaking the ferns and shedding his jacket buttons right and left. He was all in pieces.

Moppet and Mittens tried to pull him together but his hat fell off and the rest of his buttons burst.

While they were in difficulties, there was a pit pat, paddle pat! Three Puddle-Ducks came along the road, marching one behind the other and doing the goose step – pit pat, paddle pat! Pit pat, waddle pat!

They stopped and stared up at the
kittens. Then Rebeccah and Jemima
Puddle-Duck picked up the hat and
tucker and put them on.

Mittens laughed so much that she fell off the wall. Moppet and Tom tumbled after her.

The pinafores and all the rest of Tom's clothes came off on the way down.

"Come Mr Drake Puddle-Duck!" said Moppet. "Come and help us to dress him! Come and button up Tom!"

Mr Drake Puddle-Duck advanced in a sideways manner and picked up the various articles. But he put them on himself! They fitted him even worse than Tom Kitten!

"It's a very fine morning," said
Mr Drake Puddle-Duck.

And he and Jemima and Rebeccah set
off up the road keeping step – pit pat,
paddle pat! Pit pat, waddle pat!

Then Mrs Tabitha Twitchit came down the garden and found her kittens with no clothes on.

She pulled the kittens off the wall, smacked them and took them back to the house.

"Just look at you! My friends will
arrive in a minute and you are not fit
to be seen. I am affronted!" said
Mrs Tabitha Twitchit. "Go straight to
your room and not one sound do
I wish to hear!"

When her friends arrived she told them that the kittens were in bed with measles, which was not true.

Quite the contrary. They were not in bed, not in the least.

Somehow there were very extraordinary noises heard overhead, which disturbed the dignity and repose of the tea party.

As for the Puddle-Ducks, they went into a pond. The clothes came off directly because there were no buttons.

And Mr Drake Puddle-Duck, and
Jemima and Rebeccah have been
looking for them ever since.